D0624835

Kai-lan Loves YeYe!

nickelodeon

ni hao, kai-lan

adapted by Mickie Matheis
based on the screenplay "Kai-lan's Big Surprise" written by Sascha Paladino
illustrated by Kellee Riley

Simon Spotlight/Nickelodeon
New York London Toronto Sydney

Based on the TV series *Ni Hao, Kai-lan!*™ as seen on Nick Jr.™

5201 1524 6/13

SIMON SPOTLIGHT/NICKELODEON
An imprint of Simon & Schuster Children's Publishing Division
1230 Avenue of the Americas, New York, New York 10020

For information about special discounts for bulk purchases, please contact Simon & Schuster
Special Sales at 1-866-506-1949 or business@simonandschuster.com.
Manufactured in the United States 1210 LAK
First Edition 10 9 8 7 6 5 4 3 2 1
ISBN 978-1-4424-1331-3

Ni hao! I'm Kai-lan! My grandpa, YeYe, is showing me how to write in Chinese. Look—I wrote the word "love." Do you want to know how we say "I love" in Chinese? *Wo ai.* Now you try. Say "*Wo ai.*" Super!

I love so many things! *Wo ai* . . . flowers! *Wo ai* . . . ladybugs! *Wo ai* . . . YeYe!

I really love YeYe. He does so many nice things for me and our friends. Hey, I have an idea! We can have a thank-you party for YeYe! Do you think he'd like that? Yeah, so do I! Let's go tell our friends. *Gen wo lai*—follow me!

Rintoo, Tolee, and Hoho are really excited about having a party for YeYe. They want to make decorations. But first we need to figure out what color YeYe likes.

YeYe's picking apples for us. Look at his sweater and his bag and his ladder. What color are they? Right—they're red! Do you think YeYe likes the color red? I think so too. Now we know what color to use—*hong se*. Red!

Tolee's going to paint red streamers for the party. Hoho wants to paint a picture of a big red apple for YeYe. And Rintoo is making some paper flowers. YeYe will love all of it! This party is going to be super special!

Uh-oh! The red paint is all gone. Now Hoho can't paint a red apple for YeYe. Poor Hoho! He looks so sad. How can we make Hoho feel better?

Rintoo says we should give Hoho a hug. *Bao-bao*—hug-hug! Our hugs made Hoho feel a little better. But he's still sad. What else can we try to make Hoho happy?

I know! When you feel sad, do something that makes you happy. Dancing makes Tolee happy. Roaring makes Rintoo happy. Making silly faces makes me happy. What makes *you* happy? Oh, that's super!

What makes Hoho happy? Jumping! *Tiao, tiao, tiao*—jump, jump, jump! Now Hoho feels a lot better. He says he's going to paint a green apple for YeYe instead.

RAAAARR!

There are still lots of things to do to get ready for YeYe's thank-you party. We need to get some yummy treats and make a card and put up the decorations. Will you help us? Super!

Ni hao, Mr. Fluffy! We're having a thank-you party for YeYe and we need something yummy to eat. YeYe really likes pineapples.

Mr. Fluffy has a pineapple cake for YeYe. Mmmmmm—YeYe will love it! *Xie, xie*, Mr. Fluffy! This party is going to be super special!

Now we have to make a card for YeYe. Here's a picture of YeYe and me holding hands. It's perfect! I'll glue the picture to the card. Now I'll write "love" in Chinese. YeYe showed me how! Do you think YeYe will like the card? I think so too!

The decorations look beautiful! *Zhen bang*—great job! I can't wait till YeYe sees everything!

Oh, no! The wind blew down all of our decorations! It ripped YeYe's card in half. And it knocked YeYe's pineapple cake to the ground! The wind messed up everything. YeYe's party is ruined! I feel so sad. I feel like crying!

Rintoo, Tolee, and Hoho give me hugs to make me feel better. *Bao-bao*—hug-hug! Hugs are really nice. They *do* make me feel a little better.

Now Rintoo, Tolee, and Hoho are making silly faces. They remembered that making silly faces makes me feel happy.

When you feel sad, do something that makes you happy. I start making silly faces too. I feel much better now.

But how can we fix YeYe's thank-you party? I've got it! We can take the messed-up decorations and make something new for YeYe. We just have to figure out what YeYe would like.

What shape is YeYe making with his apples? Yeah—a heart! YeYe loves hearts! Let's take the decorations and make them into a big red heart for YeYe. Ooooh—it's beautiful!

And look—Mr. Fluffy brought some fresh pineapple. *Xie, xie*, Mr. Fluffy! YeYe will love it! Now we have decorations and something yummy to eat. Let's go, go, go get YeYe!

"What is this?" YeYe asks.

I tell YeYe that it's a thank-you party for all of the nice things he does. I give him an extra-big hug. *Bao-bao*—hug-hug!

"*Bu ke qi*—you're welcome," YeYe says. "You made such a wonderful party with so many of my favorite things. I love it!"

"And I love you, YeYe. *Wo ai ni*."

Thank you for helping make YeYe's party really special—and for making me feel better when I was sad. You are such a good friend. You make my heart feel super, super happy! *Wo ai ni*—I love you. *Zai jian*—good-bye!